W9-AZG-033

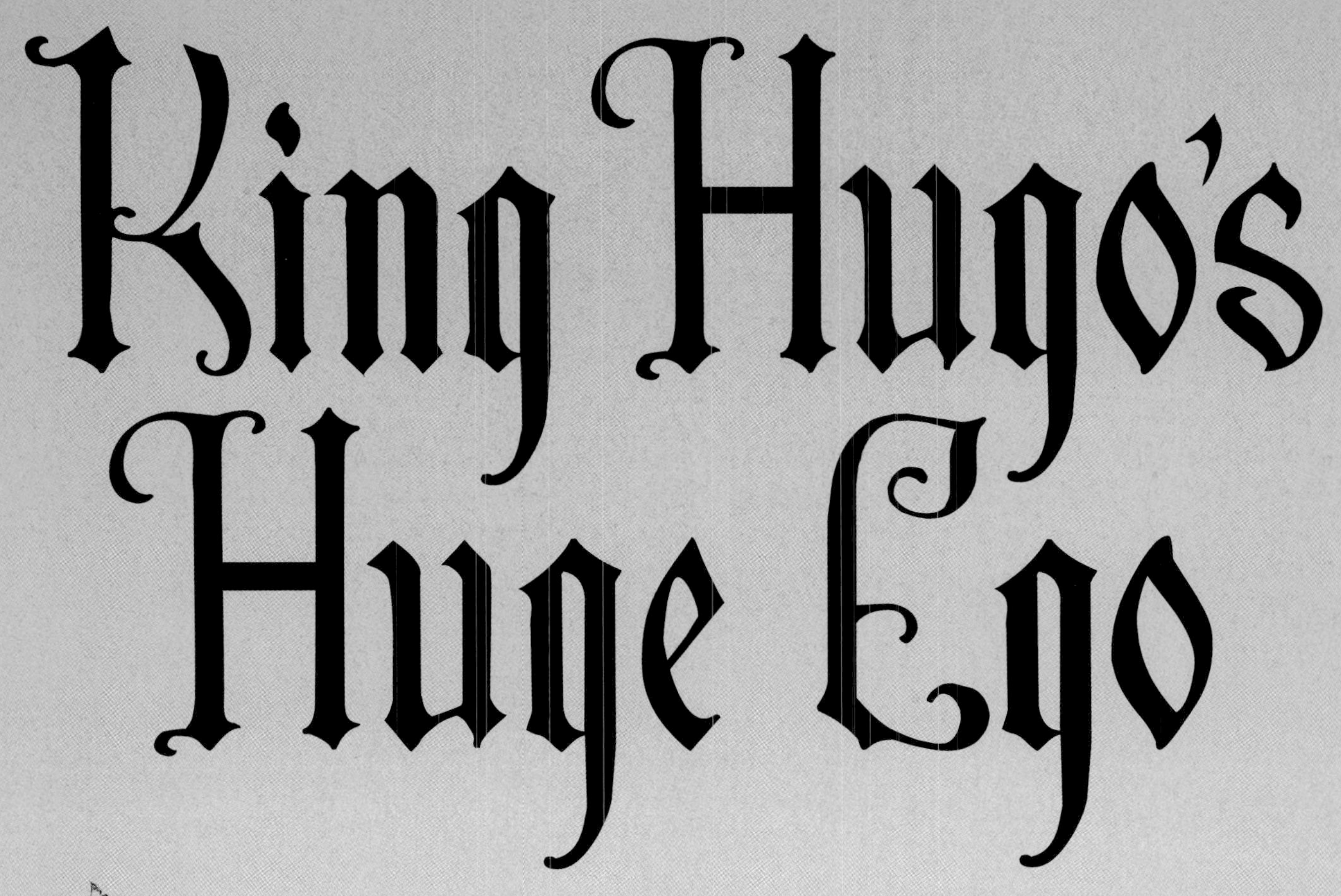

CHRIS VAN DUSEN

CANDLEWICK PRESS

Long ago, when people spoke
with words like "thou" and "thee,"
there lived a king named Hugo
who was only three foot three.

And though this mini monarch
stood no higher than an elf,
his ego was enormous—
he thought highly of himself.

Yes, Hugo was a cocky king—
as boastful as could be.
To him, no other person was
as wonderful as he.

He made his subjects bow to him
whenever he was nigh.
It pleased him to look down on them
each time that he went by.

And every Friday morning
at precisely half past ten,
his guards called all the people to
the tower base and then

King Hugo cleared his throat and gave
his captive congregation
a lengthy talk he liked to call
the Speech of Adoration.

For hours, the poor villagers
endured the boring buzz
of how mighty and magnificent
King Hugo thought he was.

One day King Hugo climbed aboard
his coach of gleaming gold
to watch the peasants bow to him
as down the road he rolled.

But when he turned a corner
by a field of amber hay,
a maiden with a heavy load
was blocking up the way.

The heralds blew their trumpets,
then called out to the lass,
"Step aside and bow your head!
Allow the king to pass!"

The girl (whose name was Tessa)
said bluntly, "Go around."
She didn't want to drop her load
and bow down on the ground.

The king began to rant and rave
and spout and spit and sputter!
"ROLL ON!" he barked, and then they bumped
poor Tessa to the gutter!

She landed in a rivulet.
Oh, what a muddy mess!
But little did King Hugo know,
she was a sorceress,

the kind with special powers
like a wizard or a witch,
so she cast a spell upon the king
while mired in the ditch.

"A pox on you, O cocky king
in robes of ruby red.
Let's see if all your arrogance
can fit inside your head."

The next day when the king awoke,
he climbed down from his bed
and gazed into his looking glass
admiringly and said,

"I do believe, dear Hugo,
you're more handsome than last night."
But when he put his crown back on,
it felt a little tight!

Then he donned his crimson robe,
the one with ermine fringe.
"How grand I am!" the king exclaimed,
then felt a little twinge.

His crown seemed even tighter now,
yet Hugo didn't care.
He hollered from his window
to the people in the square,

"Say, who's the most majestic king?
'Tis I, you must admit."
But when he pulled his head back in,
it almost didn't fit!

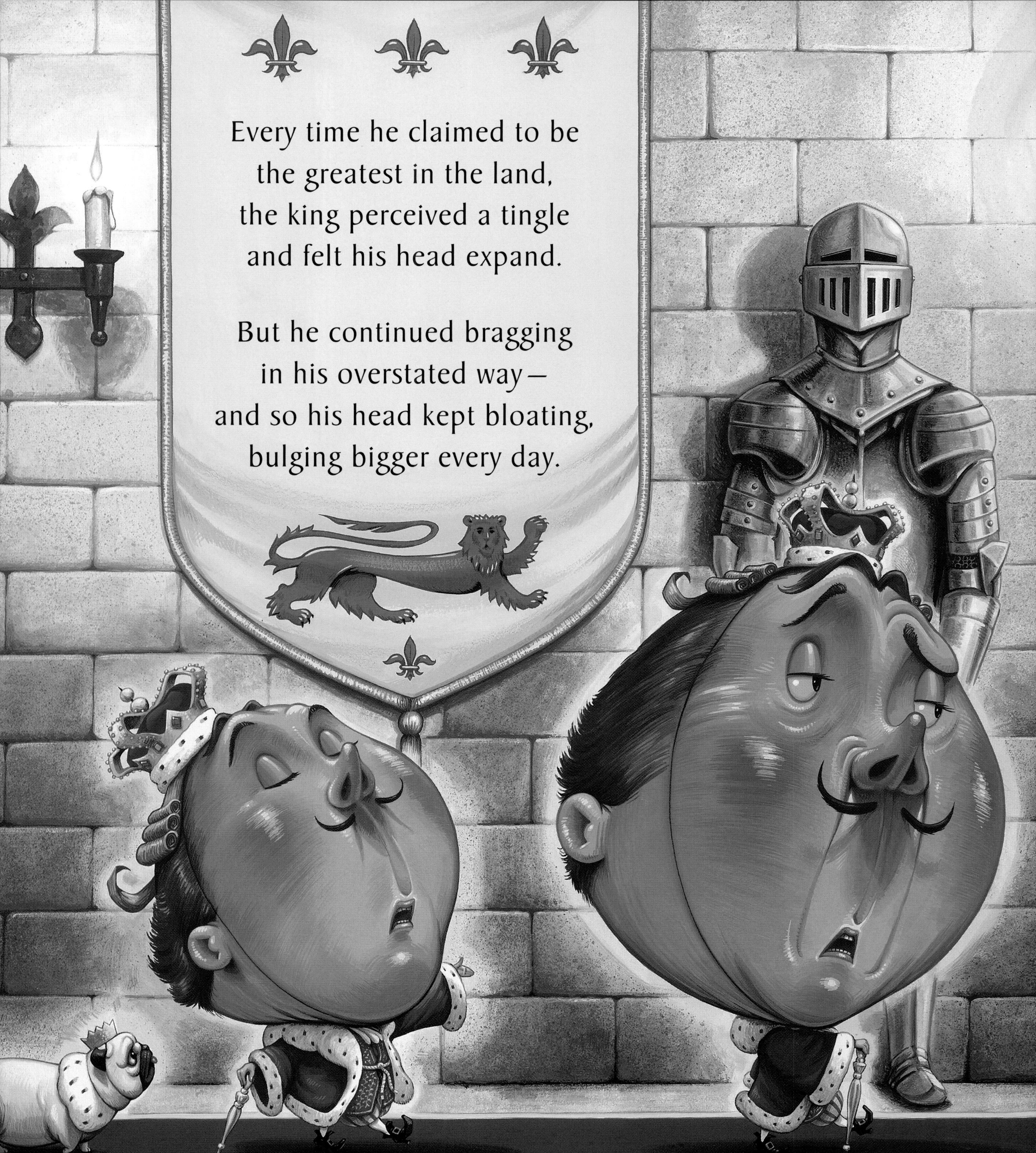

Every time he claimed to be
the greatest in the land,
the king perceived a tingle
and felt his head expand.

But he continued bragging
in his overstated way—
and so his head kept bloating,
bulging bigger every day.

By Friday, Hugo's head was huge,
but still he didn't know
that his self-directed compliments
had caused his head to grow.

His Speech of Adoration
was scheduled as before,
but when he reached the tower,
he could not fit through the door!

He marched across the courtyard
to climb the open stair,
then called the people to the wall
and gave his speech from there.

“Behold, my lowly subjects,
and do not doubt thine eyes,
for yea, my noble noggin
has increased tenfold in size.

“I know not how this happened,
but now there’s even more
of your absolutely fabulous
King Hugo to adore!”

The more he talked, the more he grew,
till suddenly a squall
hit the king's gigantic head
and pitched him off the wall!

He floated freely through the air,
then landed with a thud!
He bobbed and dipped and flipped and skipped
and toppled through the mud!

He tumbled topsy-turvy
as he bounced along the lane . . .

and ended up by Tessa,
who was busy stacking grain.

King Hugo's head was spinning.
He felt dizzy, dazed, and beat.
But when he noticed Tessa,
he yelled, "GET ME TO MY FEET!"

Tessa wandered over.
"Unbelievable," she sighed.
"Did you ever stop and wonder
why your head is ten feet wide?

"It's your ego. It's annoying!
So I cast a little spell,
and every pompous thing you've said
has caused your head to swell."

"That's ludicrous! Ridiculous!
PREPOSTEROUS! INSANE!
I'm humbler than ANYONE!"
the king snapped in disdain.

"I'll prove it to you," she replied.
"You've been this way for years.
Just listen!" ordered Tessa,
then she grabbed and tweaked his ears.

Suddenly, a blast of air
exploded from his head,
along with all the haughty things
King Hugo'd ever said!

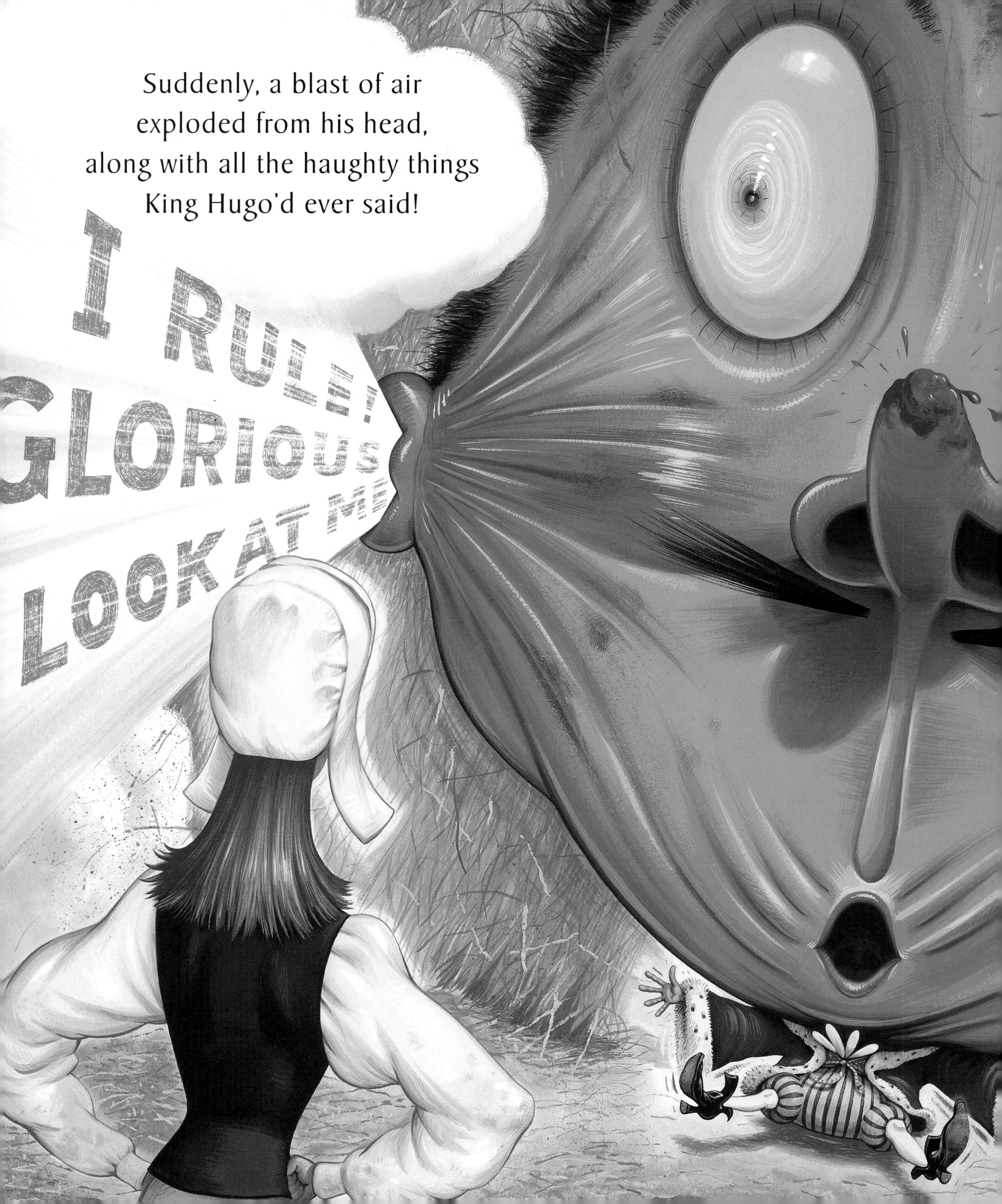

BOW DOWN
PRAISE ME
I'M SO
MAGNIFICEN

King Hugo's head deflated
like a giant pink balloon,
and when he heard what he had said,
he felt like a buffoon.

Sheepishly he said to her,
"I do apologize."
Then he looked at Tessa
with his big, sad puppy eyes.

Their glances met and instantly
she felt her heart go ZING!
Could it be, deep down inside,
she kind of *liked* the king?

The king got up. He took her hand
and bent down on his knee.
He gazed at her with tenderness,
then spoke most humbly.

"Your spell has opened up my eyes.
I've been unkind and rude.
Please stay with me and teach me how
to change my attitude."

What happened next was kismet
yet truly unforeseen:
he became a better man,
and she became a queen!

They ruled the kingdom kindly
in a fair and friendly way,
and everyone lived happily
forever and a day.

— The End —

TO NINA GRACE, A LITTLE GIRL WHO CASTS A BIG SPELL

First edition 2011

Library of Congress Cataloging-in-Publication Data

Van Dusen, Chris.
King Hugo's huge ego / Chris Van Dusen. —1st ed.
p. cm.
Summary: When haughty King Hugo tangles with a sorceress, she causes him to see himself in a more realistic light.
ISBN 978-0-7636-5004-9
[1. Stories in rhyme. 2. Kings, queens, rulers, etc.—Fiction. 3. Blessing and cursing—Fiction. 4. Egoism—Fiction. 5. Self-perception—Fiction.] I. Title.
PZ8.3.V335Ki 2011
[E]—dc22 2010040458

11 12 13 14 15 16 SWT 10 9 8 7 6 5 4 3 2 1

Printed in Dongguan, Guangdong, China

This book was typeset in Cygnet.
The illustrations were done in gouache.

Candlewick Press
99 Dover Street
Somerville, Massachusetts 02144

visit us at www.candlewick.com